T0198825

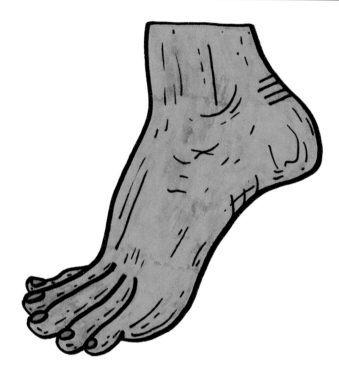

First View Of A Daspy

Rattarupphkot emerged inside
an untouched realm.

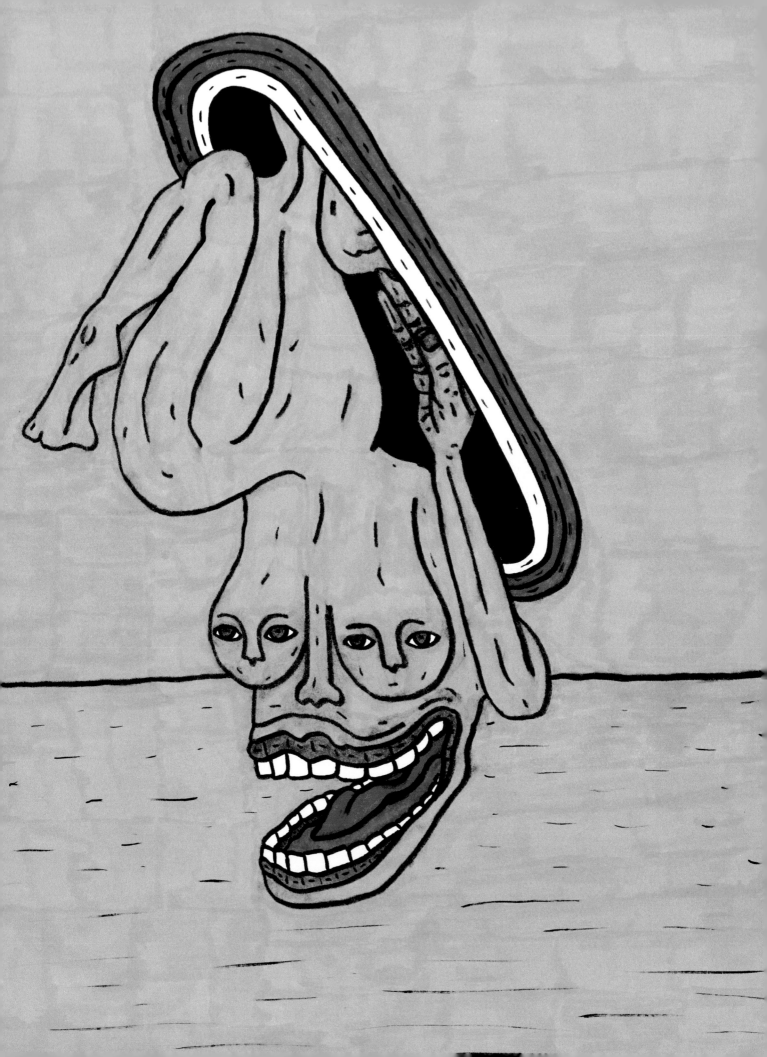

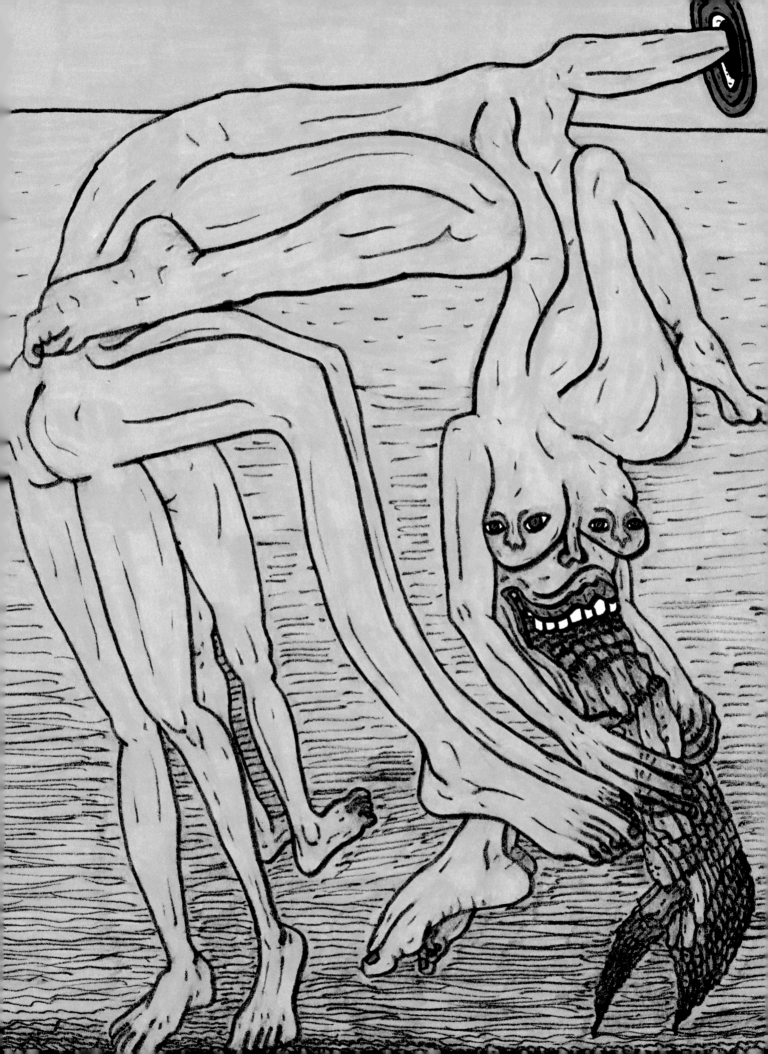

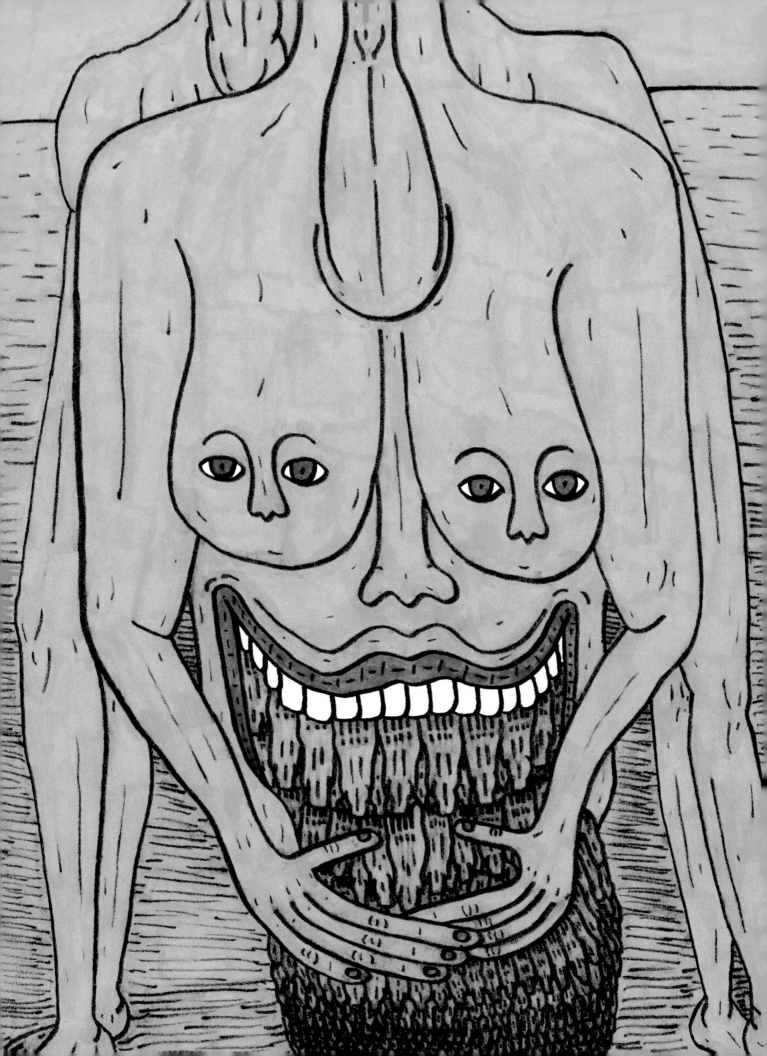

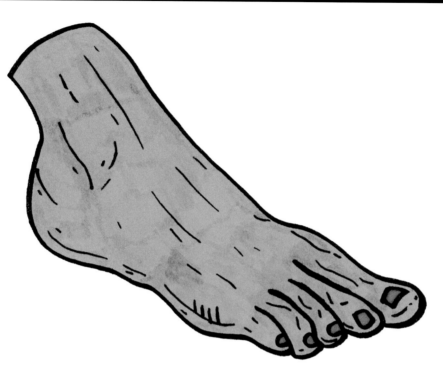

Second View Of A Daspy

Staring far out into the distance,
she desired to reach the horizon.

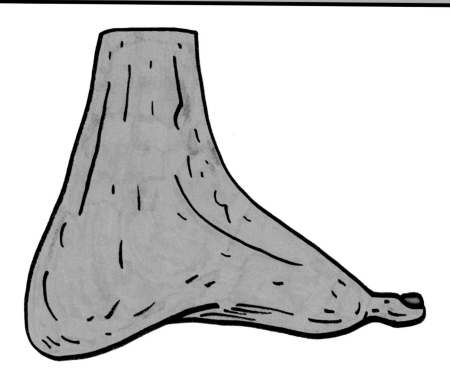

Third View Of A Daspy

So she traveled relentlessly for a
very long time until her portal no
longer could be seen.

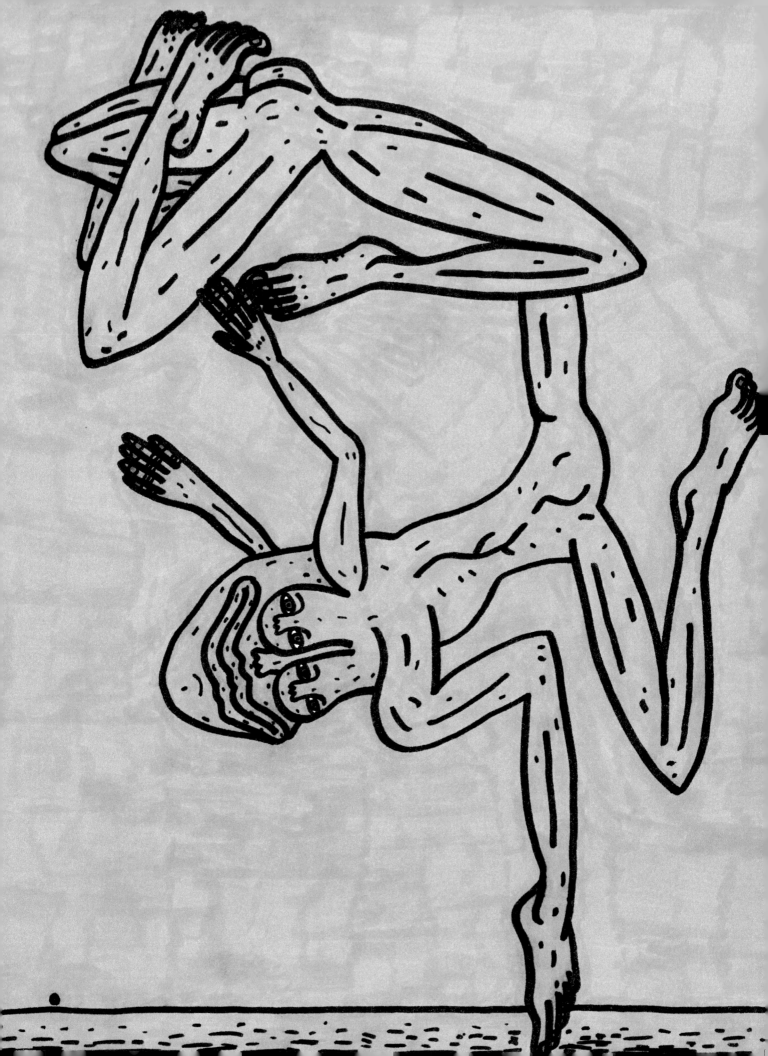

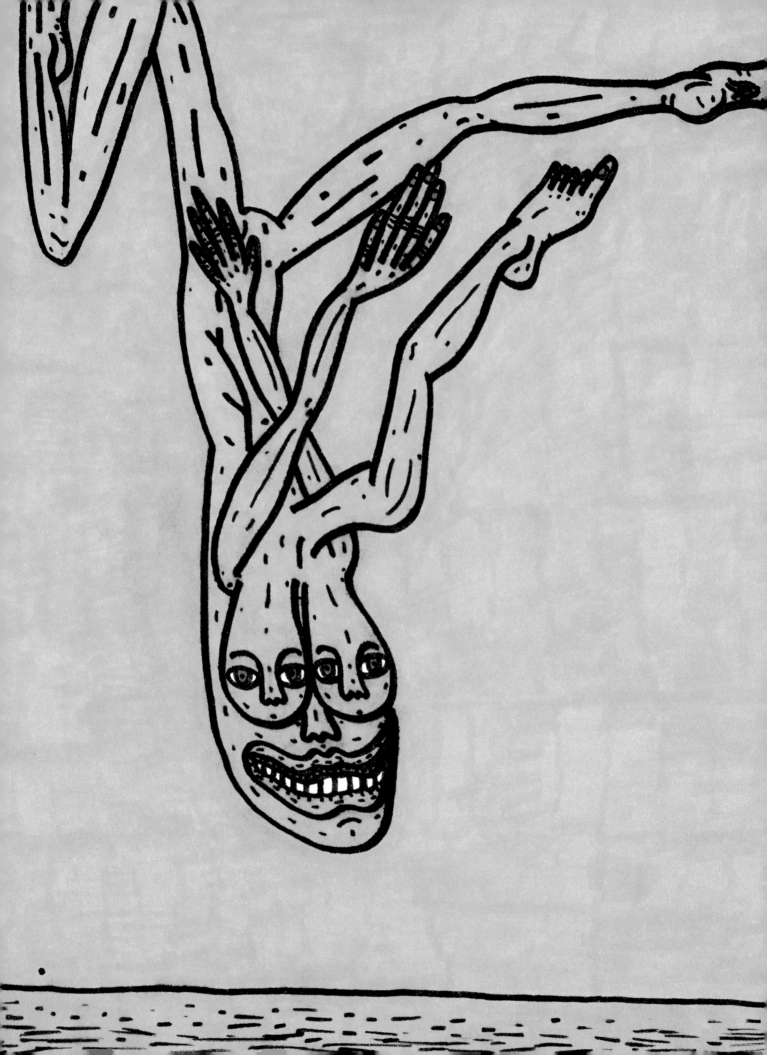

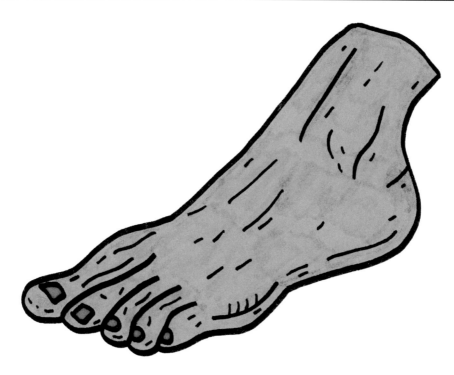

Fourth View Of A Daspy

And then the Royal Exporter met the
Eye Opener who awakened her to
the true sheer size of this place.

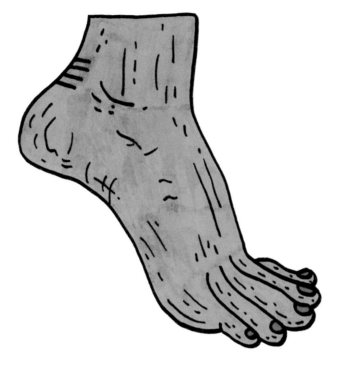

Fifth View Of A Daspy

Rattarupphkot realized that the horizon was infinitely beyond her grasp and that the number of horizons inside this realm was unlimited; each infinitely separated from all the others.

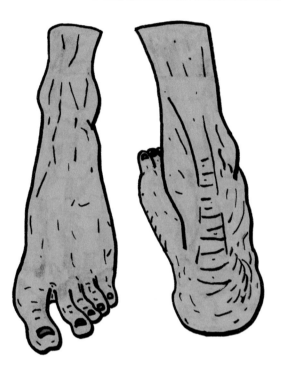

Views Of Daspies

Astonished, she named the remarkable
territory Varrungkhet, Limitless Horizons.

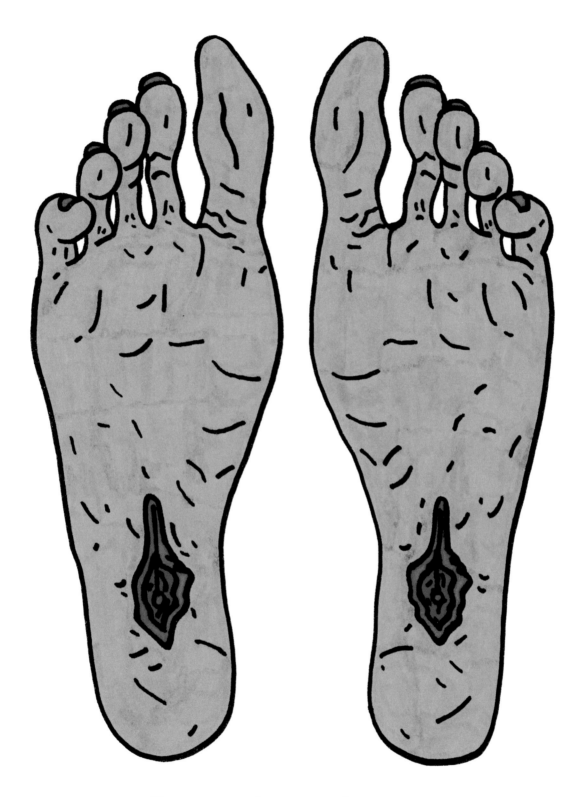

Bottom View Of Daspies

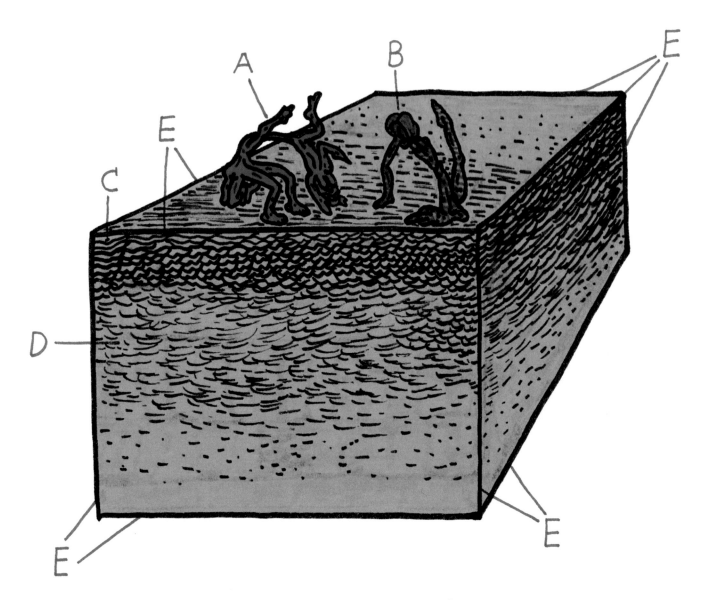

Paninfinite Paradigm Of A Veppy

A. Royal Exporter
B. Eye Opener
C. Daspy
D. Endless layers of delectable-daspies
E. Horizon

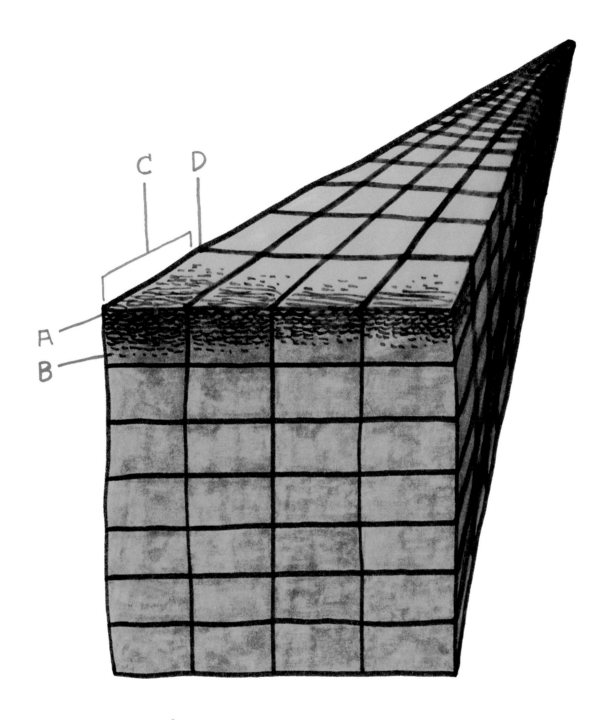

Paninfinite Panorama Of Veppies

A. Daspy
B. Endless layers of daspies
C. Infinite distance between horizons
D. Horizon

Order this book online at www.trafford.com
or email orders@trafford.com

Most Trafford titles are also available at major online book retailers.

 www.trafford.com

North America & international
toll-free: 844 688 6899 (USA & Canada)
fax: 812 355 4082

Our mission is to efficiently provide the world's finest, most comprehensive book publishing service, enabling every author to experience success. To find out how to publish your book, your way, and have it available worldwide, visit us online at www.trafford.com

Because of the dynamic nature of the Internet, any web addresses or links contained in this book may have changed since publication and may no longer be valid. The views expressed in this work are solely those of the author and do not necessarily reflect the views of the publisher, and the publisher hereby disclaims any responsibility for them.

ISBN: 978-1-4251-7649-5 (sc)

Print information available on the last page.

Trafford rev. 03/04/2021

Printed in the United States
by Baker & Taylor Publisher Services